CW01052177

A TEMPLAR BOOK

Produced by The Templar Company plc,
Pippbrook Mill, London Road, Dorking, Surrey RH4 1JE, Great Britain.

This edition produced for Parragon Books,
Unit 13-17, Avonbridge Trading Estate, Atlantic Road, Avonmouth, Bristol BS11 9QD

This book contains material first published as
The Enchanted Slippers in Enid Blyton's Sunny Stories
and Sunny Stories between 1926 and 1953.

Illustrated by Maggie Downer

Printed and bound in Italy

ISBN 1 85813 367 X

Enid Blyton's

POCKET LIBRARY

THE ENCHANTED SLIPPERS

Illustrated by Maggie Downer

PARRAGON

Once upon a time there was a boy called
William, who lived with his mother at the foot of
some high hills. Nobody lived up on the hills for it
was said that dwarfs lived in caves there, and no
one liked to walk on the sunny hillside.

William's mother often warned him not to go wandering in the hills, and to beware of any strange thing that he saw for fear it was enchanted. But William saw nothing at all, and he wasn't a bit afraid of dwarfs, no, nor giants either. Not he!

One day he went to look for wild strawberries at the foot of the hills. They were hard to find but, just as he was about to give up, he suddenly saw a sunny bank, just a little way up the hill, where he was quite certain he would find some.

To get there he had to cross a very boggy piece of ground – and dear me, before he knew what was happening he was sinking right down in it!

Quickly, William slipped off his heavy boots, which were held tightly in the mud, and leapt lightly to a dry tuft of grass.

"Bother!" he cried, "I've lost my boots! I shall get thorns and prickles in my feet if I'm not careful."

Then he saw a strange sight – for on a dry flat stone just in front of him there was a pair of fine red slippers with silver buckles! William stared at them in surprise. Who could they belong to? He looked around but he couldn't see anyone.

"Hello! Is anybody about?" William shouted loudly. "Whose shoes are these?" But there was no answer at all.

William looked at the shoes again. It seemed a pity not to borrow them when he had none. He wouldn't spoil them – he would just wear them home and then try to find out who the owner was.

So he picked up the shoes and slipped them on his feet. They fitted him exactly.

William thought they looked very nice. He stood up and tried them. Yes, they really might have been made for him!

"I'd better go back down the hill," he thought, suddenly. "I've come too far up, and mother always warns me not to."

He turned to go back down – but to his surprise his feet walked the other way! Yes, they walked *up* the hill, instead of down!

William couldn't believe it. Here he was trying to walk down the hill and he couldn't. He tried to force his feet to turn round but it was no good at all! They simply wouldn't!

"Oh no!" said William. "Why did I meddle with these shoes? I might have guessed they were magic! I've got to go where the shoes lead me, I suppose. I wonder, though, if I could take them off."

But his feet wouldn't stop walking long
enough for him to try, so on he had to go.
Up the hill his feet took him, along
a steep path, and up to a small
yellow door in the hillside.

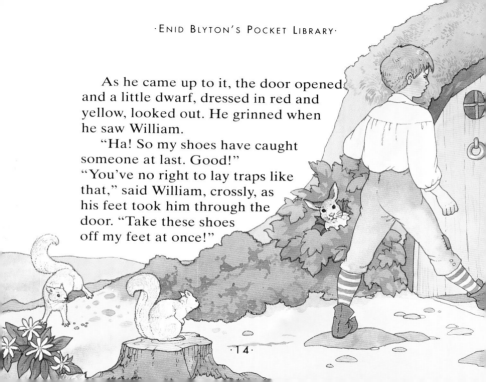

As he came up to it, the door opened, and a little dwarf, dressed in red and yellow, looked out. He grinned when he saw William.

"Ha! So my shoes have caught someone at last. Good!"

"You've no right to lay traps like that," said William, crossly, as his feet took him through the door. "Take these shoes off my feet at once!"

"Oh, no, my fine fellow!" said the dwarf, chuckling. "Now I've got you, I'm going to keep you. It's no good trying to get those shoes off – they're stuck on by magic, and only magic will get them off!"

"Well, what are you going to do with me?" asked William.

"I want an errand-boy," said the dwarf. "I do lots of business with witches, wizards and giants, sending out all sorts of spells and charms – and I want someone to deliver them for me."

"I don't see why I should work for you!" said William. "I want to go home."

"How dare you talk to me like that!" cried the dwarf, flying into a rage. "I'll turn you into a frog!"

"All right, all right!" said William, with a sigh. "But I shall escape as soon as I possibly can."

"Not as long as you've got those shoes on," said the dwarf, with a grin. "They will always bring you back to me, no matter where you go!"

Poor William. He had to start on his new job straight away!

The dwarf wrapped up a strange little blue flower in a piece of yellow paper and told William to take it to Witch Twiddle. The shoes started off at once and, puffing and panting, William climbed right to the top of the hill where he found a small cottage, half tumbling down. Green smoke came from the chimney and from inside came a high, chanting voice. It was the witch singing a spell.

"Come in!" she called when William knocked at the door. He went inside and found Witch Twiddle stirring a big black pot over a small fire. She was singing strings of magic words, and William stood open-mouthed, watching.

"What are you gaping at, nincompoop?" said the witch, impatiently.

"I'm not a nincompoop!" exclaimed William.
"It's just that I've never seen boiling water send
up green steam before!"

"Then you *are* a nincompoop!" said the witch.
"What have you come here for anyway?"

"I've come from the dwarf down the hill,"
said William. "He sent you this."

He held out the little yellow package,
and the witch pounced on it greedily.

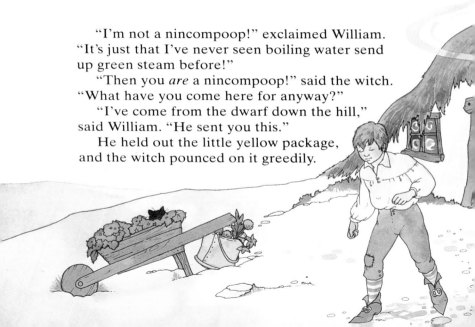

"Ha! The spell he said he would give me! Good!" William wanted to sit down and have a rest, but the enchanted slippers walked him out of the cottage and down the hill again.

Trimble the Dwarf was waiting for him with a heap of small packages to deliver.

"Look here!" said William, firmly, "I'm not going to take all those. I want a rest."

"Well, you'll have to do without one," said the dwarf. "I want these packages delivered. This goes to Castaspell the Wizard, and this to Dwindle the Dwarf, and this to Rumble the Giant."

"But I don't know where they live," said William.

"That doesn't matter," said Trimble. "The enchanted slippers will take you there!"

And so they did. It was most peculiar. First they took him to a little wood, in the middle of which was a very high tower with no door. A neat little notice said "Castaspell the Wizard."

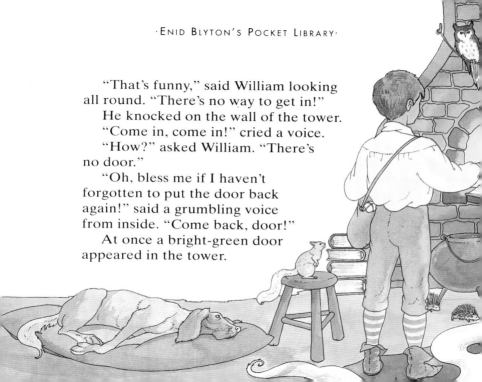

"That's funny," said William looking all round. "There's no way to get in!"

He knocked on the wall of the tower.

"Come in, come in!" cried a voice.

"How?" asked William. "There's no door."

"Oh, bless me if I haven't forgotten to put the door back again!" said a grumbling voice from inside. "Come back, door!"

At once a bright-green door appeared in the tower.

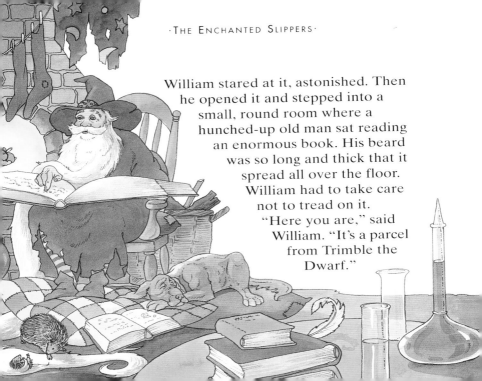

William stared at it, astonished. Then he opened it and stepped into a small, round room where a hunched-up old man sat reading an enormous book. His beard was so long and thick that it spread all over the floor. William had to take care not to tread on it.

"Here you are," said William. "It's a parcel from Trimble the Dwarf."

William gave the old man the package and left.
To his surprise the door vanished as soon as he
was outside. It was most peculiar.

His enchanted slippers would not let him stay
for a moment. They ran him out of the wizard's
wood and took him halfway down the other side
of the hill before they stopped.

"What's the matter now?" wondered William.
"I can't see any house. These slippers have made
a mistake. I hope they won't keep me out here in
the cold all day!"

Just then the earth began to shake beneath his
feet! He felt frightened, and wondered if there
was an earthquake. Then suddenly he heard a
cross little voice.

"Get off my front door! I can't open it. Get off, I say!"

The voice seemed to come from down below. William felt the earth shaking under him again – and then, to his astonishment he saw that he was standing on a neat brown trapdoor, just the colour of the hillside! On the trapdoor was a little nameplate that said: "Dwindle the Dwarf."

"I'm so sorry!" called William. "I didn't know I was standing on your front door! But my feet won't get off it."

There was an angry noise below. Then suddenly someone pushed the trapdoor open so hard that William was sent flying into the air and fell down with a bump.

"Careful!" shouted William, crossly. "You sent me flying!"

"Serve you right," said the bad-tempered dwarf, sticking his head out of the open trapdoor. "What do you want here, anyway? Are you the boy that brings the potatoes?"

"No, I am *not*!" said William. "I've been sent by Trimble the Dwarf to bring you this package."

The dwarf snatched the parcel from his hand and disappeared down the trapdoor at once, slamming it shut behind him.

"Go away," he called. "And don't you ever stand on my door again."

At once William's enchanted slippers took him back up the hill at a fast trot.

"I've only got to go to Giant Rumble now," said
William. "Thank goodness! I feel quite exhausted!"

Soon he came to something that looked like a
big golden pole. As he got near it he saw that it
was a long, long ladder of gold, reaching up into
the sky and into a large black cloud.

His feet began to climb up the ladder,
and dear me, it was very hard work!
Before he was very far up he badly
wanted a rest – but the enchanted
slippers wouldn't stop.
Up and up they went!

After a long while
William reached the
top. He looked round

and saw an extraordinary
palace, which seemed to be
made entirely of mist.

"This doesn't look as if
it is the home of a giant,"
said William, to himself.
"It's big enough – but it
doesn't seem strong enough!
It's all so soft and misty!"

But all the same, a giant *did* live there. The front door opened as William drew near, and inside he saw a great hall, higher than the highest tree he had ever seen. Sitting at a carved table was a giant with a broad, kindly face. He looked down smilingly at the boy as he walked forward.

"Where do you come from, boy?" he asked.

"From Trimble the Dwarf," answered William. "He sent you this parcel."

"About time too," said the giant, stretching out such an enormous hand for it that William felt quite frightened. "Don't be afraid, my boy. I won't hurt you. I'm a cloud-giant, and I live up here to make the thunder you hear sometimes. But I do no harm to anyone."

The giant opened the parcel and then frowned angrily. "The dwarf has sent me the wrong spell again!" he grumbled. "Do *you* know anything about spells, boy?"

"Nothing at all," said William.

"Dear me, that's a pity," said Rumble. "I'm doing a summer-thunder spell, and I've got to multiply twelve lightning flashes by eleven thunder claps. I don't know the answer. Trimble said he'd send it to me, but he hasn't, I'm sure."

"What does he say the answer is?" asked William, who knew his tables very well indeed.

"He says that twelve flashes of lightning multiplied by eleven claps of thunder make ninety-nine storm-clouds," said Rumble.

"Quite wrong," said William. "Twelve times eleven is one hundred and thirty-two."

"Well, is that so?" said the giant. "I *am* pleased! Now I can do my spell. I'm really very much obliged to you. I suppose I can't possibly do anything for you in return?"

"Well, yes, you can," said William, at once. "You can tell me how to get rid of these slippers."

"Well, the only way to get rid of them is to put them on someone else," said Rumble. "Tell me who you'd like to put them on and I'll tell you how to get them off!"

"I'd like to make that horrid little Dwarf Trimble wear them, and send him off to the moon!" said William.

"Ha, ha, ha, ha!" laughed the giant. "Best joke
I've heard for years! That would serve him right.
Now listen. Wait till the dwarf is asleep, and then
slip these tiny stones into your slippers. You will
find that they come off at once. Put them on
Trimble's feet before you can count ten, and tell
him where to go. He'll go all right! The slippers
will start him walking and he'll never come back."

"Oh thank you," said William gratefully
and took the small pebbles that Rumble
gave him. He said goodbye to the
kindly giant and then climbed
quickly down the ladder.

He was soon back at Trimble's house and found
him having his dinner. The dwarf threw the
boy a crust dipped in gravy and told him
that as soon he had finished eating there
were some more errands to do.

"I'm going to have my after-
dinner nap," he said, lying
down on a sofa. "Wake me
when you've finished
cleaning up."

William was too excited even to eat his crust. As soon as he heard Trimble snoring loudly William slipped the magic pebbles into the slippers. They came off as easily as could be, and in great delight he ran over to Trimble. As soon as the slippers were off, William began to count.

"One–two–three," he counted, as he began to slip the shoes on to Trimble's feet – but to his horror the dwarf's feet were far too large – twice the size of William's! Whatever could he do?

"Four, five, six, seven, eight, nine—" he continued to count in despair, for the shoes certainly would *not* go on the dwarf's feet. And then, at the very last moment William had an idea. He would put them on the dwarf's hands!

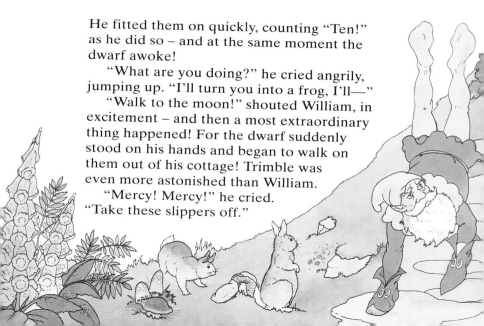

He fitted them on quickly, counting "Ten!" as he did so – and at the same moment the dwarf awoke!

"What are you doing?" he cried angrily, jumping up. "I'll turn you into a frog, I'll—"

"Walk to the moon!" shouted William, in excitement – and then a most extraordinary thing happened! For the dwarf suddenly stood on his hands and began to walk on them out of his cottage! Trimble was even more astonished than William.

"Mercy! Mercy!" he cried. "Take these slippers off."

"I don't know how to," said William. "But anyway, it serves you right. Go on, slippers – walk to the moon and then, if the dwarf has repented of his bad ways, you may bring him back again!"

The dwarf was soon a long way off, walking upside down on his hands, weeping and wailing.

As soon as the dwarf was out of sight a crowd of little folk came running up to William. They were dressed in red and green tunics and had bright happy faces.

"We are the hill-brownies," they said, "and we've come to thank you for punishing that horrible dwarf. Now we shall all be happy, and you and your friends can walk safely up the hillside. Ho ho! Wasn't it a surprise for Trimble to be sent walking to the moon on his hands! That was very clever of you."

The jolly little hill-brownies took William safely back home, and even fetched his lost boots for him out of the bog into which they had sunk. And now William and his friends walk unafraid all over the hills, for the friendly brownies are about now and the nasty dwarfs have fled, frightened by the fate of Trimble.

As for Trimble he hasn't even walked halfway to the moon yet, so goodness knows when he'll be back!